Llama Pajamas

Early ★ Reader

First American edition published in 2023 by Lerner Publishing Group, Inc.

An original concept by Jenny Jinks
Copyright © 2023 Jenny Jinks

Illustrated by Addy Rivera Sonda

First published by Maverick Arts Publishing Limited

Maverick
arts publishing

Licensed Edition
Llama Pajamas

Lerner Publications Company
An imprint of Lerner Publishing Group, Inc.
241 First Avenue North
Minneapolis, MN 55401 USA

For reading levels and more information, look up this title at www.lernerbooks.com.

Main body text set in Mikado a. Typeface provided by HVD Fonts.

Library of Congress Cataloging-in-Publication Data

Names: Jinks, Jenny, author. | Sonda, Addy Rivera, illustrator.
Title: Llama pajamas / Jenny Jinks ; illustrated by Addy Rivera Sonda.
Description: First American edition. | Minneapolis : Lerner Publications, 2023. | Series: Early
   bird readers. Blue (Early bird stories) | "First published by Maverick Arts Publishing
   Limited"—Page facing title page. | Audience: Ages 4–8. | Audience: Grades K–1. |
   Summary: "Larry the llama's wool makes him hot. A haircut cools him down, but he is too
   cold at night. How can he stay warm when the sun goes down?"— Provided by publisher.
Identifiers: LCCN 2022020194 (print) | LCCN 2022020195 (ebook) | ISBN 9781728476414
   (lib. bdg.) | ISBN 9781728478456 (pbk.) | ISBN 9781728482101 (eb pdf)
Subjects: LCSH: Readers (Primary) | LCGFT: Readers (Publications)
Classification: LCC PE1119.2 .J564 2023 (print) | LCC PE1119.2 (ebook) | DDC 428.6/2—
   dc23/eng/20220503

LC record available at https://lccn.loc.gov/2022020194
LC ebook record available at https://lccn.loc.gov/2022020195

Manufactured in the United States of America
3-1010767-50662-3/11/2024

EARLY BIRD STORIES

Llama Pajamas

illustrated by
Jenny Jinks   **Addy Rivera Sonda**

Lerner Publications ◆ Minneapolis

Larry was fed up.

"I am hot!" he said.

"My wool is too thick."

"Go for a swim," said Terry.

Larry swam in the pool.

Larry's wool got wetter and
wetter, and bigger and bigger.
But he was still hot.

"Sit under the tree," said Terry.

Larry sat under the tree.

But the twigs stuck in his wool.

And he was still hot.

"I can help," said Edna.

SNIP!

SNIP!

SNIP!

"You look odd," said all the llamas.

But now Larry was not hot.

He was not wet. He did not itch.

"I like my short hair," he said.

But when the sun went down,

Larry got cold. He began to shiver.

"I miss my wool," he said.

Larry was fed up.

But Terry had a plan.

"Put your wool back on," said Terry.

Larry got his wool and put it back on.

But the wool did not stick.

"Brrrrrr," Larry said.

He was still cold.

"I can help," said Edna.

She took Larry's wool.

"What are they?" said all the llamas.

"You look odd."

But now Larry was not cold.

"I like my pajamas!" he said.

Now Larry ran in the sun and swam in the pool.

And when it got cold, he was snug in his pajamas.

"I wish we were like Larry," all the llamas said.

"Can you help us too?" the llamas
said to Edna.

"Yes!" said Edna.

SNIP! SNIP!

CLICK! CLACK!

Now all the llamas had short hair.

And they all had a . . .

...LLAMA PAJAMA PARTY!

Quiz

1. What is Larry?
   a) A llama
   b) A dog
   c) A cat

2. What happens when Larry goes for a swim?
   a) He gets cold
   b) His wool gets bigger and bigger
   c) He gets hot

3. "I can help," said _____.
   a) Terry
   b) Ben
   c) Edna

4. Why does Larry feel cold?

    a) Because the sun went down

    b) Because his wool is sticky

    c) Because Terry has pajamas

5. And when it got cold, he was _____ in his pajamas.

    a) Hot

    b) Snug

    c) Cold

EARLY BIRD STORIES™

Leveled for Guided Reading

Early Bird Stories have been edited and leveled by leading educational consultants to correspond with guided reading levels. The levels are assigned by taking into account the content, language style, layout, and phonics used in each book. Visit www.lernerbooks.com for more Early Bird Readers titles!

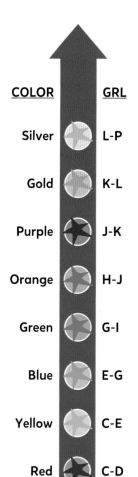

COLOR	GRL
Silver	L-P
Gold	K-L
Purple	J-K
Orange	H-J
Green	G-I
Blue	E-G
Yellow	C-E
Red	C-D
Pink	A-C